Rudolph Jr. Misses the Roof

A Daxton and Miranda Adventure!

Written by: **David W. Trapp**

Illustrated by: **Lou MacGregor**

R.R.P.

Trapp Family Publishing LLC

Rudolph Jr. Misses the Roof

ISBN 978-0-9800946-7-1
ISBN 0-9800946-7-4

This book, additional titles, stuffed toy animals, and accessories based on *Daxton and Miranda Adventure Books* can be found at:

MYINJUREDPET.COM

Other Books Written by
David W Trapp:

A Conservative Terrorist:
  The Demise of Walter Reed

Plates of Gold and Other Spiritual
Poems

The Donkey and the Elephant

The $45,000 Cat

"Miraculous Majesty Flies Again"
A Daxton and Miranda Adventure

"Tipsy Russell Recovers"
A Daxton and Miranda Adventure

"Army Dill Gets Shelled"
A Daxton and Miranda Adventure

"Kitty Gets Leveled"
A Daxton and Miranda Adventure

"Tom Turkey Gets Pardoned"
A Daxton and Miranda Adventure

Dedication: *This book is dedicated to my mother; thanks Mom for all you have done for me.*

Daxton and Miranda are a young brother and sister who reside in Utah, and they love animals. They do not just love any animals; they love animals that have been hurt or injured in any manner. The two siblings have saved the lives of the American National Symbol and a young Jack Russell Terrier they had received for Christmas the previous year.

They also saved an armadillo during a visit to their Uncle David's ranch in Arizona.

During the previous Halloween they rescued "Kitty" from a group of teenage boys bent on torturing an Abyssinian cat.

During the following Thanksgiving holiday they were recognized by the President of the United States for their life-saving efforts.

Their prominent recognition included a pardoned Tom Turkey which they are now raising on their Utah farm.

———————

This is the story of how Daxton and Miranda, with the assistance of Santa Claus and some magic dust, were involved in helping Rudolph Jr. (Santa's latest Red-Nosed Reindeer) recover from a tragic accident:

Daxton and Miranda could hardly wait for the following day; tomorrow was Christmas, and they were as excited as two young siblings could be. This year was the year that Miranda had asked for a "Tipsy Russell" stuffed toy animal that was offered by the MyInjuredPet.com website.

"I can't wait," she told Daxton for the umpteenth time.

Daxton smiled at her and replied, "I know sis." He was very patient with his sister and they shared a special bond, especially when they were saving animals together.

Miranda wanted to be a veterinarian when she grew up and already had a sizeable collection of stuffed animals that sported injuries of different kinds.

Daxton loved animals as well, and had a few stuffed toy animals of his own, but he was more concerned about rescuing live animals than he was about saving animals that he could not help.

"I'm just excited that MyInjuredPet.com liked our idea about the dog" he said. "Maybe they can also make one of Miraculous Majesty."

Miraculous was an American Bald Eagle and the very first animal that Daxton and Miranda had saved; little did they know, but MyInjuredPet.com was already in the process of creating a new stuffed toy animal based upon that raptor.

Daxton stretched his arms high and looked at his mom and dad who were sitting comfortably together on the nearby couch. Daxton's mom was snuggled next to his father as they both watched a Christmas Special.

"I think I'm going to go to my room and do some research, and then go to bed" Daxton told them.

"That's fine," Mom Sharp told her son. "Miranda?" she questioned.

"Yes mom?" she returned the query.

"Are you ready for bed as well?"

"I'm too excited," she told her mother. "I want to stay up and see if I get a *Tipsy Russell* or not".

Dad Sharp laughed and told his daughter, "I don't think so, little girl. You need to get on upstairs to bed."

"Okay, Dad" she replied.

"Be sure to brush your teeth before bed, both of you," said Mother as she looked at her two offspring. "But, first let's have our family prayer."

After their prayer, Daxton and Miranda both stood up from where they had been kneeling; giving their parents hugs and kisses, the two youngsters headed up the stairs to their bedrooms.

"Dibs on the bathroom," called out Daxton as he took off up the stairs.

"Me first," yelled Miranda as she ran quickly behind him, attempting to overtake his lead. They both ran up the stairs as fast as they could.

Later, Daxton lay in his bed and contemplated the previous year. The entire year had been both exciting and busy; he and Miranda had saved a number of animals and he had grown a little older, and a little wiser.

Daxton had even met the President of the United States, and had also gotten to know the President's son, Bruce. He knew that he and Bruce would be life-long friends.

As he closed his eyes and allowed sleep to overcome him, he smiled to himself and wondered what Santa Claus would bring him for Christmas.

Soon, he was sound asleep.

Daxton woke with a start. He sat up in his bed and looked around. What was that strange noise that he heard? He listened quietly and just when he was ready to settle down again, and thinking that it was just his imagination, he heard a voice coming from outside his window.

"Oh dear, dear, what am I going to do? Oh my, oh my, oh my." Someone sounded like they were in trouble.

Daxton continued listening alertly, wondering if it was his vivid imagination taking hold.

Once again, he heard the voice. "Oh Rudolph Jr., please wake up."

Daxton sprang up from his bed and stumbled to his window. Pulling the curtain back, he put his face close to the window and peered outside. Below on the front lawn he observed one of the strangest scenes ever witnessed.

Daxton squinted mightily, blinking his eyes a number of times in disbelief. There below him he viewed the backside of a large man wearing a red suit trimmed in white, the man was bent over a dark, motionless form lying on the ground.

Stretching out in front of the man were seven reindeer hooked to a huge brown, polished sleigh.

In the sleigh was a large brightly colored bag with packages poking out of the top.

"Santa Claus?" breathed Daxton in disbelief. *"Seriously?"* He had just recently quit believing in the magical creature although he still secretly wondered if the 'fat man' was real or not.

Most of Daxton's friends were adamant that there was no such thing as Santa Claus.

Now he had living proof right here on his own front lawn that Santa was real!

Daxton turned away from the window and quickly walked towards his closed bedroom door. He quietly opened the door and stepped through. He quickly crossed the hallway and lightly tapped on Miranda's door. Impatiently, he stood before her door and waited for a reply. Hearing no response, he knocked again a little louder; he still heard nothing.

Giving a small grunt of exasperation, he slowly turned the knob, and pushed open the door.

"Miranda," he quietly called out as he entered her bedroom. "Miranda?"

He slowly inched his way towards her bed, in the dark room he was careful not to trip over anything on the floor. His knee mad contact with her bed, now that his eyes were adjusting to the dark, he could make out her small body lying under the covers, so he inched his way around the side of the bed.

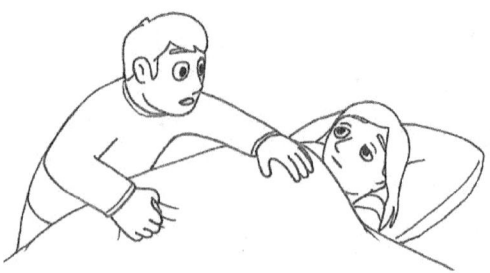

Reaching down, he shook her through the covers and called her name again. "Miranda, wake up," he said.

Miranda stirred under Daxton's shaking. "What? What's wrong?"

"Shhh," he said. "Get up, I have something to show you."

"Come on Dax, it's the middle of the night."

"I know," he replied. "But, you have to see this. Hurry!"

Miranda grumbled "Okay, okay." She threw back her covers and climbed out of bed. "This better be good."

"It is, it is," he whispered excitedly. "Believe me, it is!"

He turned around and led the way out into the hallway.

Both children quietly made their way down the stairs, the bright moonlight shining through the skylight over the stairway. When they reached the bottom step

Daxton took Miranda's hand and very quietly told her, "Now, be quiet, we don't want to scare them."

"Scare who?" she whispered back.

"I will show you." He pulled on her hand and led her towards the bay windows in the living room that overlooked the front of the house.

Daxton slowly and carefully pulled back the heavy, brown curtains just enough to allow them to see out into the front yard. He pulled Miranda close and placing his arm around his sister's shoulders guided her to the front window. "Look there" he breathed quietly into her ear.

She gave a little gasp as she realized what he was showing her. There in front of her stood Santa Claus, nine reindeer and a sleigh.

She paused and counted again, there was only eight reindeer. "What the heck?" she thought to herself. "Where is Rudolph?" It was then that she noticed Santa was just standing there in the front lawn, slowly shaking his head; she realized that he was doing so while at the same time obscuring a still form on the ground.

Realizing the possibility that a reindeer could be hurt, she called out in a quiet voice "I think Rudolph is hurt." She looked again, "Come on Daxton, let's go see if we can help!" The two children turned as one and walked quickly to the front door. They opened the door and peered out. Santa still did not notice them, so they walked towards him.

"Santa?" Daxton called out.

Startled, Santa gave a jump,
turned around and saw the two
children.

"Hi Daxton, Hi Miranda," he
gestured at them with a wave. "I
think I have a problem."

Daxton and Miranda started
forward trying to peer around
Santa.

"How do you know our names?"
asked Miranda.

Santa Claus ushered them forward while replying, "I know every little boy and girl. That's my job, right?" He looked at them with twinkling eyes.

"I did not think you were real," Daxton spoke up.

"My friends told me that you were just make-believe" he continued.

Santa gave a hearty chuckle. "Well, here I am," he said. "Do I look make-believe to you?"

"No," admitted Daxton. "You don't".

"Sometimes your friends may think they are smart, but obviously, they don't know everything." Santa told him as he turned back to the reindeer resting uncomfortably on the ground.

"You two children have had an interesting year," Santa Claus continued. "You have saved a few animals that have needed your help."

Turning around to face them he asked, "Do you think maybe you can help me save another? Rudolph Junior is in bad shape."

The two children edged their way past Santa and sank to their knees next to the inert form of a full-sized reindeer with a dully shining red nose.

"It's Rudolph," whispered Miranda.

"Yeah," Daxton said, "and he is hurt!" He looked up at Santa Claus with wondering eyes.

The fat man in the bright red suit, looked back at Daxton and then explained to the two children who now stood up.

"Well, you know that this isn't really Rudolph, right?" He looked at them both and then continued.

"This is actually the great, great grandeer of the very first Rudolph; we call him Rudolph Junior number six, and we call him Junior for short. But, even Junior here is no longer as young as he used to be." Santa looked at the two children to see if they understood.

The two children nodded in acceptance as Santa continued, "Even with his regular dose of magic dust it seems as if he isn't quite up to the difficulties of a one-night trip around the world. As he tried to land on your roof, his front hooves made it, but his back hooves missed. The sleigh was just too heavy and it pulled us all down. The other reindeer were able to adjust, but Rudolph Jr. just could not handle it."

Santa moved forward and knelt down over the quiet reindeer, joined by Daxton and Miranda.

"So, what can we do?" Daxton queried.

"Well, I can't give him another dose of magic dust until he is able to drink it with water, and I don't have a water dish or water to give him anyway."

"I can help," exclaimed Miranda. "We have all that stuff." The young girl took off for the front door with Daxton and Santa watching in surprise.

"Well," said Santa in a bemused manner. "I guess she wants to help!"

"Yep, she is really good with injured animals" Daxton explained.

Santa chuckled softly. "Yes, I know that" he said.

They both turned to look down at Rudolph Jr. as they heard a grunt. Junior's eyes were open and he was looking at them in a dazed manner.

Daxton kneeled by the reindeer and patted its head. "It's okay Rudolph Six, we will fix you right up."

Rudolph Junior looked at Santa Claus as if to see what he thought.

"Yes, Junior?" Santa seemed to listen for a moment and then he replied. "Yes, you are hurt, but we are getting you some magic dust and that should help you back up." Santa paused for a moment and then continued. "I don't know if it will help grow your antlers back or not, I've never used it for that particular purpose."

Santa listened again as Daxton watched. Daxton sat still listening intently, wondering what Santa was hearing; Daxton could hear nothing.

Santa began speaking again. "Well, it looks like your right front leg is broken. And, yes that does seem to be a problem." He paused for a half a second. "I'm not sure what we will do if the magic dust does not work. We are not nearly done with tonight's deliveries."

"And," he continued. "The deliveries must be made."

It was right then that Miranda returned from the house carefully carrying a big bowl filled with water.

Miranda gingerly placed the bowl close to Rudolph Junior's head where he could easily reach it.

Looking up at Santa she questioned, "What do we do next?"

Santa looked at Rudolph Six. "Well," he said. "Are you ready to give it a try?"

Rudolph Junior Number Six gave a slight nod. Santa turned towards his sleigh and walked to the rear. Pressing a button, a door located on the back of the sleigh sprang open.

Inside was a storage area with bottles and jars filled with mysteriously colored fluids.

Tucked in next to the jars was a small cloth bag tied tightly with a red bow that matched the color of Santa's suit. Santa reached in and pulled the bag out. Holding it in both hands, he walked back towards Rudolph Junior and the two young children.

"Okay you two," he said as he approached, "You both need to step back so that you do not ingest any of this dust."

As the two children stepped back, Santa continued speaking, "There is no telling what would happen if you inhaled some of this…it is powerful stuff!" The two children watched carefully as Santa knelt next to Rudolph Jr.

"Okay boy," he said softly. "I'm going to give you a pinch of this dust, and then I want you to take a good long drink of water."

Rudolph Number Six grunted in reply and carefully raised his head. Santa leaned in close to the reindeer and with his right hand took a pinch of magic dust and sprinkled it into Rudolph Junior's open mouth. The hurt reindeer swallowed slowly and then turned his head towards the water dish. Taking several sips of water, the reindeer swallowed again and again.

As Daxton and Miranda watched a soft, white ethereal type glow seemed to spread through Rudolph Jr's body. It started at the reindeer's head and as it traveled downward it lit his body with a soft brightness.

Rudolph Junior's eyes were no longer glazed and his antlers took on a more burnished and powerful look; the antlers did not grow any larger, nor did they repair themselves, but they did look much healthier.

The three humans bent over Rudolph Number Six anxiously, waiting to see what effects the magic dust would have on the reindeer's leg.

"I hope this works," whispered Santa fervently. "I don't know what I will do if Junior can't fly tonight."

Santa Claus looked at the two children standing at his side.

Suddenly Rudolph Junior snorted. The reindeer tried to stand, but his leg did not work correctly.

"Hold on, Junior," cautioned Santa. "Your leg does not look as if it is fully healed yet."

Indeed, as Daxton and Miranda watched, Rudolph Junior's leg strengthened itself, and an audible crack could be heard as the leg bone came together. Junior shook his head and again tried to stand. This time, the leg was stronger, and he was able to bear his own weight as he stood.

"Well," commented Santa, "At least his leg is healed." Santa Claus reached out and unhooked Rudolph Junior's collar. "Now let's see if he can fly."

The red-nosed reindeer looked at Santa and shook his head back and forth.

Santa asked him, "You don't think you can fly?"

The reindeer shook his head in a negative manner once again.

"I can't give you more magic dust," Santa told the creature. "More than two doses in one night can cause harm that cannot be undone."

"Two doses?" questioned Daxton.

"Yes," replied Santa. "At the start of every Christmas Eve journey, I give each of the reindeer a dose of magic dust to help them fly for a longer period of time than they can normally fly. Otherwise, they would not be able to make the entire trip around the world."

"Oh." Daxton nodded his head in understanding.

"So," interjected Miranda, "If you gave him one more dose, it would overload him?"

"I think so," replied Santa.

"The only other time I gave any of the reindeer a triple dose was when Prancer smacked into a chimney, and the reason I think he did that was because the two previous doses was too much for him."

"Why did you have to give him two doses?" inquired Daxton.

"That was a strange night," Santa told them. "Prancer took his normal dose before we began, but about halfway through our trip, he misjudged a rooftop and got his eye gouged by a television antenna. That was back in the time before cable." Santa shook his head as if to clear it of those memories before he continued. "So, I gave him a second dose to repair the damage. It worked, but maybe not as good as it should have."

Santa paused for a second before continuing. "Just as we were about to complete our trip, Prancer smacked head-first into a brick chimney. I quickly gave him a third dose of magic dust, but it had the opposite effect to what I wanted."

Santa paused. "Instead of making Prancer better, it made him grow old, right before my very eyes."

"What did you do?" asked Miranda breathlessly.

"He had enough power to get to the local zoo, we had to leave him there." Santa Claus wiped away a tear from his eye, remembering one of his favorite reindeer. "He was a good reindeer, and a fine friend."

Santa took a tremulous breath and turned back to Rudolph Junior.

Placing his hand on the reindeer's shoulder he quietly asked, "How you feeling Junior?"

Junior number six looked at Santa and shook his head again.

"Well," said Santa, "I guess we will just have to take him to the zoo and leave him there until he can fly again."

"Wait a minute," said Daxton, "Could Rudolph stay here with us? We have plenty of room out back."

"I guess that could work," replied Santa. "Rudolph, what do you think?" Santa looked at Rudolph who was enthusiastically shaking his head in agreement. "Well, I guess that is a yes!" laughed Santa. "What am I going to do for a lead reindeer now?" he asked.

Miranda looked at Daxton and Santa before commenting. "Why don't you take Daxton with you? He can help you navigate, and I will keep an eye on Rudolph while you are gone." She looked at them both anxiously.

"Perhaps by the time you return, he will be all better and be strong enough to fly home," she finished speaking.

Santa looked at the two young siblings and slowly shook his head. "That just might work," he remarked. "What do you think Daxton? Would you like to be my navigator tonight?"

"Wow!" responded Daxton. "That would be awesome!"

"Then that is settled," announced Santa Clause. "Miranda, Rudolph? You two will be okay?" he asked.

Miranda placed her arm across Rudolph Junior's back in a protective manner and said, "We will be just fine!"

Santa laughed as Rudolph agreed with Miranda.

"Daxton," Santa said, turning to the young boy, "Let us be on our way, we have a lot of deliveries to complete and time is ticking on."

Daxton eagerly climbed up into the large sleigh and settled himself down on the comfortable bench. "What do you want me to do?" he asked Santa.

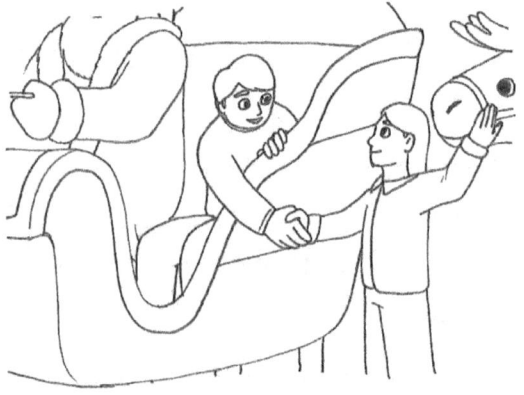

Santa clambered up into the sleigh next to Daxton and then pressed a button on the dashboard.

"We are going to use the back-up GPS to track which houses to go to, where the good boys and girls are. Your job will be to keep me on track. Can you do that?" Santa asked Daxton.

"Yes," replied Daxton, "I am very familiar with computers and research."

Santa laughed and said, "Yes, I bet you are."

Santa and Daxton settled into their seats, as Santa took the reins into his hands. "Okay, Thorne and Dirk, you two are my leaders now, let's see how you do."

The two lead reindeer looked back at Santa and gave him a vigorous head shake. Turning back towards the front, they lifted their front legs and with a concerted powerful push off their back legs pulled the sleigh into the air.

Daxton gave a yelp of excitement and held on tight to the inside side rail. Looking at the GPS monitor installed in the sleigh's dashboard, Dax told Santa, "We need to stop at the next house down the road, it's Nic and Cole's house. I guess they have been pretty good this year."

Santa laughed. "Let's just say, they could have been better." Both Daxton and Santa laughed out loud.

The remainder of the night passed by in a blur for Daxton; as he grew more comfortable with the GPS system and the quick movements of Santa and the sleigh, he grew more confident of himself and was able to provide directions in a measured manner.

As the sun began to peek over the mountain tops, Santa, the eight reindeer, and Daxton returned to the Sharp household. Santa guided the sleigh to the ground in the backyard where Miranda and Rudolph Junior Number Six where standing together, waiting for their return.

When the sleigh came to a full stop, Daxton quickly jumped out and ran to his sister. "It was so cool!" he told her. "I helped Santa deliver all his presents, and we did not get lost even once."

Miranda smiled at Daxton. "Well," she said, "Rudolph Junior and I had a great time as well, didn't we Rudolph?"

Rudolph Jr. nodded his head vigorously in agreement. The reindeer looked at Miranda with an excited expression.

"And guess what?" continued Miranda. "Rudolph can fly!"

Santa clapped his hands in delight. "Really?" he asked Rudolph.

Junior stepped away from Santa and sprang up into the air, where he hovered for a moment before slowly gliding back to the ground.

"That's wonderful!" Santa exclaimed; turning to the two children standing in front of him, he continued.

"I don't know how I can thank you" he told them. "You have just helped me save Christmas for millions of little boys and girls. Thank you, thank you. Now tell me, what it is that you most want for Christmas."

Almost before the words were even out of his mouth, Miranda spoke up with alacrity. "I want a stuffed toy Tipsy Russell animal."

Santa laughed out loud. "Why doesn't that surprise me?" he asked rhetorically. Reaching across the seat of the sleigh, he burrowed into his bag of presents and pulled forth a white and brown Jack Russell Terrier stuffed animal that was missing his left front paw, and had an eye patch covering his left eye.

The animal was an exact replica of the little Jack Russell Terrier that Daxton and Miranda had saved from almost certain death the previous Christmas. Santa handed the stuffed toy animal to Miranda, who grabbed it and clutched it to her chest.

"Thank you, thank you Santa," she breathed out. "I love it."

Santa chuckled and turned to Daxton. "Young man? What do you most desire for your Christmas present?"

Daxton was quiet for a moment and then replied.

"I would like an Asus, VivoBook X540SA 15.6 Laptop with 4 gigabits of memory and a 500 gigabit hard drive." Daxton finished with a flourish and looked at Santa expectantly.

Santa laughed out loud and said, "I think I can help you out there Daxton." He again reached into his now depleted gift bag and pulled out a silver laptop computer. "Is this what you wanted?" he questioned.

"Wow! Yes, that's it exactly" Daxton reverently replied. Daxton took the computer into his hands and opened it carefully. "Thank you, Santa, this is awesome!" Dax looked at Santa Claus with happiness glowing on his face.

"You are welcome young man" Santa replied.

"And now it is time for us to go home. It has been a long, difficult night and I'm sure that you two children are tired as well." Santa looked at Rudolph Junior Number Six and asked, "Are you ready for the trip home Junior?"

Rudolph nodded his head in affirmation.

"Then let's get you hooked up, boy." Santa and Rudolph Junior walked to the front of the sleigh where Santa settled him into his traces. After he was done, Santa climbed into the sleigh, grabbing the reins in his hands he cried out, "Time to go, Rudolph, Thorne, Dirk, are you guys all set?"

The nine reindeer all snorted and nodded their heads.

"Then let's go, on Donner, on Cupid, on Beto, onward, onward, up, up and away!"

The reindeer all heaved forward as one unit, and jumped into the air, Santa's sleigh easily lifting off. The ensemble floated in the air above the two children as Santa looked down upon them.

"Daxton. Miranda. Thank you once again for all your help. I will remember you always!"

Daxton and Miranda raised their hands and waved goodbye. They stood in the yard waving slowly as the sleigh quickly disappeared into the early morning sky.

Finally, the sleigh was no longer visible. Turning towards the house, and carrying their gifts, the brother and sister walked to the front door. They softly opened the door and entered their domicile.

Walking to the stairs, they were soon at their bedroom doors.

The two siblings looked at each other and smiled, they had saved another animal, but this time no one would ever know.

_____

It was Christmas morning; Daxton woke to see the early sun shining softly through his bedroom window. Suddenly he remembered the activities from the previous night.

Quickly he jumped out of bed, grabbed his robe and hurriedly put it on over his pajamas. He rushed to his sister's bedroom and lightly tapped on the door.

"Miranda?" he called out.

"Come in," she replied. Daxton opened the door and rapidly walked across the floor to his sister's bed.

He plunked himself down and said "So, what do you think sis?"

Miranda looked at him in surprise. "Do you mean about Christmas?" she asked.

"No, you know what I mean," he replied. "About last night, Rudolph, Santa Claus?"

"What are you talking about," she asked as she looked at him in a puzzled manner.

"You know, you know! We saved Rudolph, I went with Santa, you stayed here and nursed Rudolph Junior back to health. Santa gave us gifts."

Miranda shook her head in disbelief.

"Oh, Daxton. You are absolutely crazy. Either that, or you had a very strange dream."

Daxton sat back for a second. "You mean, it did not really happen? Wow, it seemed so real."

Miranda laughed. "Well, Santa may have left us gifts, but, we will have to go downstairs to see." She jumped out of bed, and led the way to her doorway.

Daxton contemplated her backside for a second before he jumped up and chased after her. The two young children raced down the stairs where Miranda found a new stuffed Tipsy Russell toy animal, and Daxton discovered a brand-new Asus laptop. It wasn't until much later that Mom Sharp found an envelope tucked in among the stockings hanging from the fireplace.

It was unaddressed so she opened it; inside was a hand-written letter.

"Dear Daxton and Miranda," she read. "Thank you for your efforts in saving hurt animals. May your efforts always have positive results." The letter was signed *S.C.*

The End